Short Tales From a Tall Person

Copyright ©2012 by Sun Dragon Press Inc.
All Rights Reserved

No part of this publication may be reproduced or transmitted in any form or by any means, electronic or mechanical, including photocopy, recording or any information storage and retrieval system without the written permission of the author.

Disclaimer:
All characters in this book are fictitious, and any resemblance to actual persons, living or dead, is purely coincidental.

Cover Art by Carly Hatton

Author Photo: Icon Photography

Library and Archives Canada Cataloguing in Publication

Editor: Laura LaRocca and Gloria Nye

ISBN: 978-0-9877607-3-9

Printed in United States of America

Published by Sun Dragon Press Inc., Canada
www.sundragonpress.com
First Edition, 2012

Short Tales From a Tall Person

A Thoroughly Mixed Bag of Prose and Poetry

by

Marilyn Kleiber

SUN DRAGON PRESS INC.

DEDICATION

To Robert, my husband, who has always been my greatest supporter.

Marilyn Kleiber

ACKNOWLEDGMENTS

My thanks to friends who encouraged me to publish these stories, to two wonderful editors, Laura LaRocca, Gloria Nye for their help in honing the writing and making sure I had given my readers enough information. They all convinced me people reading my stories might not be aware of exactly what is hidden in my brain that could be germane to the stories.

Thanks too, to the other writers at the Headwaters' Writers Guild for the prompts that triggered many of these stories.

I also am so appreciative of the internet and being able to research anything almost instantly, and of course, the absolutely vital help from my own special IT professional, Sharon Bennett.

Finally very special thanks to an extraordinary young woman, Carly Hatton, who produced the cover drawing for this book. She captured my-tongue-in-cheek title perfectly.

Marilyn Kleiber

NO POSTAGE
NECESSARY
IF MAILED IN
THE UNITED
STATES

BUSINESS REPLY MAIL
FIRST-CLASS MAIL PERMIT NO. 1 LITCHFIELD, CT

POSTAGE WILL BE PAID BY ADDRESSEE

White Flower Farm
PLANTSMEN SINCE 1950
PO BOX 50
LITCHFIELD, CONNECTICUT 06759-9988

Give a gift to a friend!

We always enjoy meeting new friends with the same affection (or is it affliction?) for gardening that we have. If you know gardeners who would appreciate learning about our vast offering of plants, please write their names below, and we'll mail them our current catalogue with a note that it was sent by you. We'll also give them a $5 credit to use on their first order. Your friends (and their garden) will thank you!

Name _____ Address _____

E-mail _____ City _____ State ____ Zip _____

Name _____ Address _____

E-mail _____ City _____ State ____ Zip _____

Your Name (please print)

4S001

A FORWARD EXPLANATION

You are probably wondering, dear reader, why I've called this book "Short Tales from a Tall Person," when the drawing on the front cover clearly illustrates exactly the opposite.

The fault, I confess, lies with my parents. Coming from South Africa, where the only really tall people were the beautiful and regal Zulus, I was expected to be unusually tall. This, because at the age of 10, I was fast approaching my mother's grand height of 5' 2". Since my father had only reached the staggering height of 5' 9", both parents constantly exclaimed "she's going to be really tall."

Naturally I was convinced I was tall. This is a belief I hold to this day, and no six footers or higher will ever convince me otherwise. Personally those people over six feet appear to me to be freakishly vertically challenged. While I, on the other hand, am simply tall.

So how far up the scale do I go? I am 5' 3 3/8". Trust me, when you're as tall as I am, every 1/8 of an inch counts.

So whether tall or less so, I hope you enjoy this collection of stories and poems which run the gamut from comedy to horror and everything in between. Each was written in a variety of circumstances, but most often when I was firmly and happily ensconced in inspiration.

Marilyn Kleiber

I have rarely experienced writer's block, which I know creates such agony for many writers. The only times such challenges caused me distress is because I knew I was trying to force words onto paper that carried no inspiration. So now I never sit down to pour forth prose unless I am inspired. For me inspiration comes frequently because I know that creativity will always find a home within me. For this, of course, I profoundly thank the Universe.

Ah, yes, I also thank my parents for creating such a tall person.

TABLE OF CONTENTS

INSPIRATION	1
WHY?	3
GARGOYLE	7
PIRATES	11
THE FRUITS OF LIFE	13
BROTHERS	15
A LIGHT TALE	19
UNCLE HENRY	25
WHAT IS FAITH?	29
DREAM LOVER	33
FASHION DISASTER	35
A FREUDIAN CEILING	41
GROUNDED	45
THE SONGS OF LEONARD COHEN	49
DANIEL MY BROTHER	51
WELCOME TO OUR WORLD	55

SECOND CHANCE	69
THE FOREST	81
BELOVED PAINT	83
THE PROFESSIONAL	89
PUPPY LOVE	95
BLAME THE SUN	101
THE BLIND DATE	105
ENDINGS	111
THE PLANT IN THE CORNER	113
CAT	117

INSPIRATION

The lightning bolt of inspiration strikes
and it is now that words can flow
onto the still stark white of paper from
the fevered rush of images.

When I have spewed all into written form,
I marvel at what I read.
From where were these characters born?
Was it truly all my doing or
was my muse the universal all that
grants access to greatness, to tales
of human frailties, of love and crime,
and deeds most foul?

I need not know the source, but
simply revel in the fount of visions
tumbling from my fingers into
electronic permanency.

Did all greatest artists benefit from this bounty?

Did Milton 'see" all he needed,
written on the blank slate of his blind vision?

Marilyn Kleiber

Did Beethoven hear each note he wrote
inside his head, bypassing deafened ears?

WHY?

If I had a choice, I definitely would have run for cover when I saw the flash of flame. But with a blast of sound, the car shattered into thousands of shards so quickly I scarcely had time to throw myself behind the dumpster. I covered my head, unable to fathom what was happening, as concrete lumps and garbage rained down on me. When the deluge ceased, the acrid smell of smoked and burning flesh assailed my nostrils. I was too shocked to register anything but nausea.

When I finally lifted my eyes, there in front of me was Ferris, a look of surprise upon his face. As I dragged myself to my feet, my bruised and battered limbs protesting violently, I turned and retched. It wasn't Ferris—it was his head.

We had pushed someone's buttons all right, and Ferris had paid the price. I would have too if I hadn't darted back into the restaurant for my wallet.

I started violently as a man in uniform caught me by the arm, his mouth moving soundlessly. I relaxed as my addled brain told me he was a cop, but I couldn't hear his words. The explosion had deafened me completely.

I rubbed my ears into responding. They were wet. Blood covered my fingers. The explosion had broken my left eardrum and it would be some time before my hearing returned fully.

That, more than anything, sent icy tendrils of fear up my spine. I was vulnerable and someone out there wanted us dead. They had already succeeded with Ferris, poor sod.

The cop led me by the arm to an ambulance which had just arrived. Luckily, both attendants were already busy tending to more serious cases and I sidled out of their sight and escaped, staggering slightly, down the maze of alleys. I panicked, running for my very existence.

For the first time in my life, my reporter's desire to know was shrouded in deep terror. I had no idea who needed to cover their tracks enough to blow us up. What nerve had we struck that elicited such a violent response? The story had seemed so innocuous when Jackson, our editor, handed it to me. I had specifically requested Ferris as my cameraman because I trusted him in any situation, and he was good at his job.

I had caused his death. Now, in addition to a pounding head, ears like cotton wool, and gut-churning nausea, I donned the mantle of guilt. How could I ever face his wife and children?

Fear kept me on my feet and heading for cover and oblivion. Who would think a simple bit of bribery in council chambers could bring this kind of attack? It was totally incomprehensible.

I emerged from a damp, dark alley. Oh god no! In my befuddled state, I had run in a complete circle. I had to get away. I had to hide.

The same cop who first found me turned in recognition. "There you are, sir. We wondered where you had disappeared to."

I could barely discern his words. My hearing was returning. "Officer, I..." I tried to back away from him.

He caught me by the arm again. "It's okay. You're safe now, sir. It's over. It's just unfortunate that you were in the wrong place at the wrong time and got caught up in this."

"Caught up? You mean...they weren't after us?"

"No, not you sir. We suspect it was an IRA bombing. It was the vehicle ahead of yours that exploded. That car contained the British Minister for Irish Affairs."

Marilyn Kleiber

GARGOYLE

I hate pigeons!

They are the most noxious and annoying birds, and their intellectual properties do not even surpass those of streetcars.

Of course I know about streetcars. I see them rumbling past my cathedral every day. What a boring existence they must have, always running in the same direction, day in and day out.

But back to pigeons. Not only do they have the mentally stultifying effect of terminal stupidity, but they obviously have abysmal eating habits. Nothing else could possibly explain the erratic and liquid state of their bowels.

As I sit here on the edge of Notre Dame's vaulted roof, I see much of life below me. I particularly take note of the multitudes who are led about by their dogs. Dogs who, from time to time, perch coyly and with immense satisfaction on small patches of city grass to make deposits of meals long past, while their owners pretend to be absorbed in far more lofty subjects. Once the said dogs have completed their *toilette,* the dog walkers rush up with plastic coverings on their hands, scoop up the offending materials, and hastily deposit them into the nearest waste container. One would think this performance would be relegated to a particular category of humans. However, dog-walking folks run the gamut, from the working man to the dainty woman in furs. How odd these creatures are.

It is my observation of these details of daily life that allows me to draw the conclusion that, oddly enough, birds are the only creatures who evacuate in black and white.

I know you're wondering about my preoccupation with bowels, and those of feathered creatures in particular.

Perhaps as I describe my typical day, you will catch a glimmer of understanding.

The night is always peaceful on my rooftop. The air is clear and cool, and the stars are usually bright and beckoning. The world is truly my oyster at times like these. At the first blush of the dawn, however, those blasted pigeons appear.

What terrible sin did I commit in my stone age to deserve this rain of bird poop? The pigeon who always roosts upon my head has the absolutely worst case of chronic diarrhea, and by midday, I am adorned in layers of the damn stuff.

Can you imagine how it feels to have your thrusting tongue covered in guano?

Quelle horreur!

I am only free of these cursed birds when the bell tolls. How I look forward to morning mass, to evensong, to Sunday services, and especially to weddings.

It is such blessed relief from pigeon shit!

Sometimes, when it rains with enough force, I am relieved of my overcoat of crap.

When day dies into night, peace descends and again, I am on my own. Free until the morning light brings an end to my most pleasant ruminations.

Thus, this is my daily existence, locked in a timeless struggle with fowl excrement.

Is this really my eternal destiny?

Marilyn Kleiber

PIRATES

The argument had dragged on for nearly three hours. When all this was over, the secretary would have to produce notes worthy of Tolstoy to explain the total bedlam of this meeting.

They had met to decide upon a some logical ground rules for their ad hoc group, and also to lay out each sector's rights and responsibilities.

Freddy had insisted long and loudly that pirates should not be allowed to be considered part of the guild as they were malicious, sneaky, and as trustworthy as a dieting crocodile.

Jack yelled back with equal volume that the group were not discussing crocodiles. They were discussing the only other human species in the area—the pirates. He insisted that they too were people—something the rest of us did not dispute—and so should be allowed inclusion in the community. Sure, they had caused trouble under their nasty malicious leader, but he was gone. There was no reason now to exclude them from membership.

Four of five voices joined in the fray, each trying to drown out the other.

Freddie, frustrated that he was losing control of the meeting and desperate to be heard above the cacophony of sound screamed "Shut up!" and held up both hands for silence. For a brief moment you could have heard a fairy whisper.

This was just as well, because at last Tinkerbell spoke.

"You really shouldn't vote on this before Peter gets here. He will never allow pirates in the gang. Unless," she added, "you let me sprinkle them with special fairy dust to put a peace spell on all nine of them. You know what challenges he has had with them in the past."

Blessed ear healing silence followed her announcement.

From the back of the room, Peter's voice startled the entire group.

"What was that you just proposed, Tinkerbell?" he asked.

She gritted her teeth in exasperation, sending off sparks of red. *Peter never listens to me.* "I said that you would probably agree to their membership if I sprinkled all nine of them with a fairy glitter dust peace spell."

"If it doesn't work, you know they will be sentenced to banishment and probable death."

"Look, it will work. But" she added, "it must be done before midnight, because the spell has a time limit and I can only use it once, and it has to be today."

"Ah," Peter smirked, "so what you're saying is: *a spell in time saves nine*?"

THE FRUITS OF LIFE

Life is not a bowl of cherries
with undiscovered pits in hiding.
Instead, it is a fruit salad with
flavors and colors to tempt
the taste of all who live on this splendid earth.

Sometimes when I devour life,
it is a tart green apple,
replete with the raw and simple scent of heaven.
My tongue shivers in delight
and yearns for something more.

Sometimes it is watermelon
crisp and cool and liquid, so full of promise.
Slaking parched desires
and cooling heated lips
with laughter as I spit seeds in contest with myself.

But my fondest taste of life is mango,
true ambrosia, best eaten in the bath,
juices running down my arms as
I twist my body to lick my elbows
and suck last flavor from the pit.

Marilyn Kleiber

It is then I use my most playful imagination.
Flavor and scent enveloping and expanding
the sensual meaning of bliss eternal.
I draw last flesh from the strands of fruit
to create a fish that once was mango.

Children may yearn for oranges, bright in color
and bright in life, bursting juicy from their skins,
which shoot sprays of citrus-scented oil.
Often they adorn their childish ears with pairs
of red ripe cherries, plump and succulent with sunshine.

Others may find the bland and grainy pear
is all they expect from life, so indeed they
have little to excite, and much that is banal.
Or perhaps they pop the juicy grape before
it transforms to raisin in the sun.

My own life is many things, not so much
the sharp green bite of apple, nor
life-giving fluid of watermelon,
nor cherries red, nor grape so green,
but solely the sweet juicy ecstasy of mango.

BROTHERS

He tied a rope to the bag and lowered it carefully from the rear bedroom window of his brother's house into the darkness below. He turned back to the room and meticulously mopped the few spots of blood from the floor with an old, used handkerchief from his pocket. In the light from the waning moon, he picked up the picture from the dresser. He could almost hear the laughter of the three small boys they had once been. He sighed at the foolish thoughts of past happiness, and replaced the picture on the dresser.

He crossed the room and listened carefully at the door. He was grateful and amazed that Grace slept so soundly through Daneel's snoring. If she knew what they were up to, she would start spouting all those ridiculous biblical references about abominations. It wouldn't matter that Daneel was her husband, she would still carry tales to her equally rigid church friends, and he and his brother would be torn limb from limb, or even worse.

Softly, he descended the stairs, missing the creaking step, and barefooted his way out the back door, pausing briefly to pick up an old pair of sneakers. Once outside, he waited only long enough to allow his eyes to pick up the faint ambient light from the glowing cesspool at the side of the house. It had once been a source of such sweet water, but the war three years ago and the plague that followed it had poisoned so much of the planet, and their beautiful pond had been one of the many casualties. He briefly sat on the porch chair, put on the shoes, and laced them up.

Retrieving the bag from the back of the house, he set off toward the dark line of hills about a mile away. He grunted in satisfaction. The contents of the bag would feed them well tonight. It was a long walk, with little or no danger from any four-footed creatures. Most of those had died off long ago. However, the ones with two feet often proved catastrophic. He clung to the shadows of the trees.

Nearing the caves at the foot of the hills, he blew the soft whistle of a nighthawk. The answering croak of a bullfrog told him it was safe to continue.

"Arla," he whispered, "I've got supper."

He passed through a thick growth of bushes into the dim interior of the cave, lit only by the dying embers of the fire they struggled to keep alive.

A large male, dressed in rags and the badly cured skins of animals, rose from a group huddled around the fire and strode toward him, seizing him in a bone-crushing hug. "Faron. Thank the lord you've come. We're almost out of wood, and it's pretty scarce around here. With the *thumpers* patrolling, it's getting more difficult to go too far from this place."

Faron knew he meant the bible revivalists. "I left a big pile by the old oak yesterday. You can get it anytime."

The big male nodded his thanks. He took the bag from Faron and peered into it. "Another of Daneel's mistakes?"

"Yeah. He keeps trying to find the cure."

"Why does he keep doing it? It puts both of you in a terrible position."

"Don't you understand? He wants his big brother back." Faron was almost angry. "He wants you home again."

"Does he really think he's going to cure this?" Arla gestured to the half of his body that was scarred, twisted, and covered in oddly shiny scales. "He's taking foolish chances. That witch he's married to would love to find out where I am so she could sic her *thumper* buddies on me. You know I'm right."

"Yeah, I do know. He just wants us to be family again."

The big man shook his head in pity. "Then he's a bigger fool than I thought. Besides," he added, and indicated the oddly deformed group around the fire, "they're my family now."

"He's not the only one that wants the three of us together again," Faron pleaded.

"I do know that." He gazed at Faron pityingly. "But you realize that's never going to happen."

Small rustlings echoed in the cave as the rest of the clan crept forward, lured by the scent of the contents of the bag. A clawed hand snatched it from Arla's grasp, and the largest female, with little whimpering cries of hunger, ripped it open and the contents tumbled to the ground, a kaleidoscope of blonde hair, flayed skin, blood, and five-fingered, furry paws.

"Dan's little errors are looking more human these days," Arla said. "Is it?"

"Would that make a difference?"

"Not really. We will use whatever it takes to stay alive."

"Well, it may look human, but it's not." Faron turned and strode from the cave.

He stopped and turned back briefly, his eyes glistening wetly in the faint moonlight. "Enjoy your meal."

A LIGHT TALE

It's Thursday, my day for baking for the Ladies' Auxiliary when, as usual, Phil Naylor walks through my kitchen door. Phil or, as he prefers to be known, Philip Underwood Naylor, insists he is one of the literati. However, his unerring instinct for hot-out-of-the-oven cookies leads me to believe he is really a hungry mooch.

I'm not feeling particularly generous toward Phil this morning due to his recent, vicious condemnation of writers of what he refers to as "fluff." I took that particularly hard as I write the social column for our local newspaper. At least I am a published writer, while nothing of Phil's has been committed to printers' ink. He insists this is because he's still refining his great work of literary genius.

He can be quite annoying at times.

Yesterday evening, my niece amused me with the challenging question of how many people in various professions or nationalities it takes to change a lightbulb. Feeling a touch of malevolence, I ask Phil, "How many writers would it take to change a lightbulb?"

"Hmmm. I need to think about that a little but, offhand, I would say quite a few."

"Surely, Phil, based on your elevated opinion of writers' brilliance, it would only take one."

"No, no, no. It would definitely take more than one." This said, he sits on my kitchen chair, furrows his brow, and assumes the stance of a thin version of Rodin's famous statue.

At last he raises his head. "It would take seventeen writers to change a lightbulb."

My jaw drops. "How on earth did you arrive at that number?"

"Well," he says, "After much thought, I realized that to come up with an accurate number, I would have to adhere to the principles of good character, plot and story structure."

"Explain." I actually find myself begging.

"There's a story that describes it all quite well."

I could tell he was about to be lengthy, so I sit and grabbed a cookie before he could devour them all. As I sip my tea, the story unfolds.

Writer number one, the hero of Phil's story, has a ghost in his past, and an unrealized need to overcome the fear generated by this ghost. Writer one is an author of novels filled with angst.

Writer two, a member of the chorus and a playwright, comments on the onset of sudden darkness following the demise of the current lightbulb, which suffered a breakdown due to the pressure of maintaining constant light for writers who keep irregular hours.

The entire community of writers now has a pressing desire for light due, of course, to fast approaching publishing deadlines for many of the community.

Writer number three, a writer of action drama, searches the area for a new lightbulb, but none can be found in the building.

Writer four, the leader of the chorus and a prolific author of sales manuals, nominates One to locate a new bulb and install it in the place of the unfortunate previous bulb.

One will not accept the quest immediately, despite the entire community's encouragement, as he is a timid man by nature. He is also deathly afraid of heights due, of course, to the ghost in his past, but he does not yet realize that he needs to overcome this fear.

Five, the opponent and the producer of a vampire series, discusses with Six and Seven, his two equally disreputable comrades, how he intends to find the new lightbulb and install it before One is able to fulfill the task. Five wants the light first so he can submit for publication three novels he has stolen, before their authors can offer them in their own names.

Phil pauses at this point in his story for a sip of my tea and a few bites of a cookie. He meticulously wipes the crumbs from his fingers and dabs the tea from his lips before reaching for another sip.

"Go on," I say, intrigued in spite of myself.

Phil smirks and continues with the tale.

Writer number eight, a romance writer whom One secretly worships, uses techniques from her novels to persuade him. He finally, but reluctantly, accepts the quest—not because of any altruistic desire for the betterment of his community, but because of his love for Eight.

Nine, who pens a large variety of how-to books, agrees to help One by researching where new lightbulbs might be obtained.

One purchases the bulb with funds supplied by writer number ten, who regularly produces financial guide books.

Eleven, a technical engineer, locates a ladder and explains its structure and erection to One.

Twelve, an author of six mathematical manuals for graduate students, calculates the potential for success with the erection of the ladder.

Thirteen, a famous personal growth specialist, guides and mentors One in his attempts to erect the ladder directly beneath the dead, dark lightbulb.

Fourteen, a particularly well-known wordsmith, searches the thesaurus for a word to replace erection while. Five collapses the ladder in an attempt to foil One, who is now facing his darkest hour.

To keep plot and inspiration flowing, Fifteen, an editor of note, introduces a hemp-like tea ceremony that refreshes and renews One's desire. One's determination is further enhanced by encouragement from Eight.

In an act of rebellion, Seven reveals to One the reason for Five's sabotage of One's attempts at ladder erection. Alas, Fourteen was unable to locate a better word than erection.

One climbs the ladder toward his need for change and his desire for light, and finally reaches the climax of accomplishment by removing the dead, dark lightbulb and replacing it with the bright new one.

Perching on the top of the ladder, finally facing and overcoming his fear of heights, One advises the entire community of the duplicity of Five.

The community of writers sentence Five to twenty years of writing dust jacket covers for the rest of the community. They award One a contract for six books, and Eight declares her undying love for him and agrees to share her agent with him.

Sixteen, a ghost writer of excellent reputation, writes the epilogue, explaining the process of the changes, the coming of new light, and generally wraps up the story.

And Seventeen, a drama critic with an acerbic wit, critiques the entire process, which wins him a Governor General's Award.

"It almost makes sense when you put it in that way," I say when Phil returns to his cookie and tea. "So who wrote the original story?"

Phillip Underwood Naylor preens. "I did, of course."

Marilyn Kleiber

UNCLE HENRY

I can remember the exact date when Uncle Henry moved in, because that was the start of the bunch of strange happenings in our house.

First, Miss Kitty, my Siamese cat, got pregnant. No one could figure out how, because she never left the house. To add to the mystery, she was declawed and spayed.

Three weeks later, I heard a huge argument between mom and dad, which was really weird because they never yell at each other. I couldn't hear the words as the bedroom door was closed.

The next day, mom announced I was going to have a brother or sister. That was kinda gross, because mom is old! She's 58! I know I'm only eleven, but we've had those sex ed classes and even I know she was really too old to have a baby again.

The very next day, my small rabbit, Georgie had fifteen babies. This was probably the most peculiar thing of all, since the breeder had told us Georgie was a male. He could have been wrong. I guess he never actually turned the darn rabbit upside down to take a really careful look. The babies were funny looking as they had long claws on their feet for newborn bunnies.

No one thought this odd stuff was because Uncle Henry was in our house, but I could figure things out. I was not stupid.

I remembered something I had heard when I was not supposed to be listening to mom and dad last year. Mom said that since Lucy—that's me—was now ten, it was time to stop having kids. Yeah right. They should have stopped before they had my two brothers and my sister. Anyway, Dad said something about getting a vectomy or something like that. I forget the word.

Uncle Henry is really one creepy dude, and I began to get more curious about him. Was that why my parents were yelling at each other? Did he manage to sneak into my mom's bedroom without my dad knowing? Of course I know how babies are made. I told you, they covered that in Grade 5 for pete's sake. We're not dumb kids any more, you know.

Of course during the day mom was alone in the house when I was at school and dad was working, but uncle Henry was really goofy looking, so how could mom find him cool enough to do something so gross with him? He has this way of looking at you that makes you think he is sizing you up for something really nasty. His eyes also look in different directions. Even when his back is turned I always get the impression that he is still looking at me. He gives me the heebie-jeebies, big time.

Neither mom or dad believed me when I said Uncle Henry was to blame when I showed them the creepy rabbits. Dad just claimed they were an anomaly. I looked the word up in our dictionary and it said "a deviation from the norm". Yeah right! The only anomaly here is Uncle Henry.

It was the cat and the rabbit having babies that really got to me. Was Uncle Henry doing something spooky with them, like experiments or other even weirder stuff? This was really freaking me out. I'd been looking on the net, but hadn't found anything to explain it all. Every time I tried to imagine what Uncle Henry might have been doing, my spine would go all chilly, I'd get goosebumps, and all the hair stood up on my arms.

I decided to carefully examine the new rabbits. I've read about putting genes of one animal in something else. Is that what was happening? None of them resembled uncle Henry in the least, but what would a Henry/rabbit cross look like anyway? I figured he was probably some kind of alien and he could put his genes anywhere he wanted. I liked this idea much better, because then I knew mom would never have done anything with him. It was his sneaky gene thing.

I always love it when Miss Kitty figures people out. She hates uncle Henry. She hisses at him when he walks into the room and if he gets near enough she strikes out with razor sharp claws. I know if she could get close enough to him, uncle Henry would look like someone who had been run through one of those paper shredders. Cats are way cool. They know things we don't. I think Uncle Henry knows this, because he tries to stay out of her way.

Anyway, back to the rabbits. It wasn't until they were about two weeks old that I noticed the really odd thing about them. They all had black tongues and red eyes. Freaky!

When they turned about three weeks old, their mother disappeared and I saw that the babies, now full grown, had teeth like junior saber-toothed tigers. Double freaky!

It was not easy to herd them together. Those teeth were very sharp. It took some really fancy footwork, but at last I managed to pack them all into a crate and took them down to the river. It wasn't easy for me, because normally I can't even kill an earthworm, but those rabbits really scared me. I weighted the crate down with rocks and hung around just long enough to make sure there were none left alive. Whatever they were, they were not normal rabbits, and I did not regret my actions.

About this time, Miss Kitty birthed nine of the weirdest kittens. Rather than furry, sweet, and helpless babies, they were scaly and incredibly aggressive. Miss Kitty only attempted to nurse them once. I've been tending the wounds to her stomach ever since.

The kittens were dealt with in the same manner as the young rabbits. I had to, you know. They would have killed Miss Kitty and she had always been my cat, and I love her.

At this point I really became frightened. While it was tough enough destroying Miss Kitty's offspring and those of Georgie, how would I ever deal with my new brother or sister?

WHAT IS FAITH?

"I can't believe it. I gave the final draft of my book to my agent today and asked her if or when it would be published. All she'd say is that she had given it to a number of people and I just have to have faith. I'm so frustrated I could spit." Debbie waved her arms about in irritation.

"Why are you so frustrated?"

"Because I don't know what she is really saying. Faith! What the heck is faith anyway?"

"Faith is that absolute belief in the unfolding of certain events to an expected conclusion," John said. He was calmly playing sudoku with a swiftly cooling coffee beside him.

"Phooey, that sounds like a textbook answer. The real question is, how do we know that faith is justified? What proof is there?"

John squinted at the ceiling, thinking. "Well, when the events really do come about, I guess. When the events or things specifically manifest."

"John, that doesn't really tell me anything." Debbie growled at him in frustration. "You're deliberately being obtuse. Listen to me," she demanded. "For example, if someone has faith that they will go to heaven when they die, how will we know their faith was warranted?"

"Well, since they are no longer around in their physical bodies, and since it is their faith we are discussing and they have not come back to tell us their faith was misplaced, we have to assume they did, indeed, end up in heaven." He took a sip of coffee and grimaced at the taste.

"Oh, no you don't! Assumptions do not qualify as proof." She prodded him in the chest.

"Hey, be careful. I bruise easily."

"Don't be silly." Her face was pink with exasperation. "You need to prove that faith is deserved."

"Well, the facts are, people who have a strong faith that something will occur, generally do experience that outcome. They have faith that it will happen, they expect it to happen, and it does indeed come about. It's as if there is a law of expectation in effect."

"Oh, come on. How often does that really happen?" She was definitely cross with John.

"Deb, let's take a for instance. Last year you were hoping to take a trip to England, right?" He took another sip of his cold coffee, and shuddered. He pushed the cup away.

"Well, yes."

"You were so passionate about wanting to go and you were so determined it would happen, that by the time September arrived, you were on a plane to London."

"That wasn't faith. I worked my butt off at three jobs to get the money to take the trip. I would never have gone if it hadn't been for me doing all that work."

"Not necessarily true. You had an expectation that you would make the trip. You found the jobs that would help you pay your way, and you recognized the opportunities when they arose, like that special travel package for instance."

"I'm telling you, that wasn't faith, it was my detective abilities and a great deal of hard work."

John could almost see steam coming out of her nose. He sighed. "You're like a dog with a bone. Let's make it really simple. When you buy butter, where do you go?"

"To the grocery store, of course."

"Why?"

"Because, duh, that's where butter is sold."

"How do you know that?"

"Because I've bought it there before."

John grinned at her triumphantly. "I rest my case."

Deb scowled at him. "What do you mean you 'rest your case'?"

"You've bought butter there before, so now you go to there because you have faith that grocery stores carry butter!"

Marilyn Kleiber

DREAM LOVER

Like a great cat he moves
long and lithe,
silently
on great furred and padded paws
no wasted motion.
I watch.
Muscles bunch and ripple
satin over steel.
Midnight eyes pin me to place
and probe beneath my soul.
I am mesmerized.
Stillness surrounds him.
I turn away seeking control.
Silence.
When I look back
nothing but smoke remains.
Relief.
It was but fantasy and
I am released
yet disappointed.
Then on my neck hot cinnamon breath
velvet touches on my body.
Fever!
Surrender!

Marilyn Kleiber

FASHION DISASTER

Edna Mae Johansen was to fashion what Hitler was to gentle tolerance.

Today's outfit was particularly repulsive, revolting enough to make one's eyes bleed. The challenge was that her personality, unfortunately, matched her vile clothing.

We tolerated Edna Mae, although her waspish tongue, airs about being the key descendant of the first family to settle in this area, and abysmal taste in clothing did not endear her to most of the inhabitants of our small village.

However, Edna Mae was the closest thing to royalty in Silversands. When her daddy, Stanley Johansen was alive, he was the wealthiest man in the area and was, for the most part, generous to our community. He was deeply in love with his wife and built her a magnificently large, but extremely ugly, house on the highest hill in the area. All the better, he claimed, to overlook the village and the rest of his petite "kingdom." We all regarded Stanley with great affection because, unlike his daughter, he exuded love and a gentle charm for the townsfolk.

When Edna Mae was born, her mother quickly succumbed to the challenge of childbirth and was laid to rest in the family vault in the local cemetery. The unkind among us declared that she could not bear to live after the first look at her unprepossessing offspring. The truly unkind swore that Edna Mae, at birth, strongly resembled Winston Churchill which, in an elderly statesman is quite acceptable but, in a newborn, is disconcerting.

Stanley doted on his homely daughter, giving her every kind of toy the local general store carried, praising her lavishly and dressing her in the prettiest and frilliest dresses he could find. Unfortunately, nothing could disguise her fat, ungainly body, a face that could curdle the milk of the most placid cow, or those overly large hands and feet. The rest of us quickly learned to refrain from teasing her, as those hands and feet would painfully halt our words and actions with a few blows. When she realized she could control us physically, Edna Mae blossomed, rather like the plant in *The Little Shop of Horrors* and she whipped us into acting as her indentured servants with her tongue. At the age of sixteen, she threw away the frilly dresses and chose to wear suits instead. While skirts and jackets actually looked much better upon her ungainly figure, the atrocious colors and odd styles she chose turned her into even more of a caricature of a woman.

When her father went to his final rest, Edna Mae snatched greater control of the town because she now, unwittingly, contributed to our prosperity.

Silversands had once been a booming mining community and the silver capital of the entire area. Now there was neither silver nor sands, but simply a red, viscous clay that regularly captured unwary vehicles during the spring run-off. The only tourist attractions were the boarded-up mine and a dusty museum, replete with tragic souvenirs of a much heralded past.

Edna Mae persuaded the few tourists incautious enough to venture off the beaten track to dally in our dilapidated village for a short time.

Her family's large house had deteriorated over the years, but Edna Mae kept up her appearance of moneyed privilege by operating the only B & B in the area. Our few tourists were pleased enough to stay overnight at "the Manse," as Edna Mae had, in a sudden delusion of adequacy, named her crumbling home. Naturally, the longer tourists spent in "chez Silversands" as Edna Mae referred to our town, the more of their disposable income we could dispose of.

Although pretentious in the extreme, she must have been a fair business woman, as we never heard complaints from her guests, and she always had sufficient money for limited, but necessary, repairs.

About the time she turned "the Manse" into a B & B, Edna Mae obviously decided she required a clothing makeover, commensurate with her role as an hotelier. It was hard to believe that she could surpass the peculiarities of her first sojourn into suits, but she managed to wear a succession of the oddest suits ever to have seen the light of day. Most of her garments were constructed from an unusual sort of fine leather, dyed in hideous hues, and often covered in strange patterns that made no sense whatsoever. She sported jackets of washed out pinks, insipid bronzes and dusty browns. These seemed almost natural when compared with the virulent greens, pernicious yellows and eye-aching reds that were obviously the work of some psychotic colorist.

What was most peculiar was that no one in town knew where Edna Mae shopped for her clothing, and the women in my morning coffee klatch were desperate to know. We knew of no store within a hundred miles that carried the types of garments that she wore as she waddled about our streets. Oh yes, did I mention that Edna Mae was rotund in the extreme?

If the truth be known, we really didn't have much to gossip about in Silversands. Off the beaten track, shunned by most, but loved by us all, our town provided little or no entertainment. Most of the young people left at their earliest opportunity. So we created our own amusement, and the topic of Edna Mae and her bizarre attire was sufficient grist for our conversation mill.

One morning, one of our group, Carole Anne Mason volunteered to unearth the secret. She would follow Edna Mae for weeks if necessary, until she discovered the source of the horrendous clothes.

"Don't expect to see me until I come back with an answer," Carole Anne said.

She always was the bravest and most curious of women. She was the only one in town who, daringly got a tattoo. She once, after an evening of far too much wine, showed off to our coffee group, the eight inch, blue and red butterfly, forever inked upon her lower back. It was, surprisingly, quite pretty. If Edna Mae, however, had the same tattoo, it would stretch to resemble a great auk. That shuddering thought would make a strong man blanch. I think one of our number simply expressed her feelings with an "eeewww!"

Carole Anne, as a decidedly independent woman, was single. She came by this state of matrimony quite honestly as her ma, when she gave birth to Carole Anne, was also entirely single. Who Carole Anne's daddy was, we never knew, but her ma, when she was with us, and when asked about him, would give a gentle smile and a distant look of satisfaction as her only reply. In a town as small as ours, we had no place for unnecessary prejudices. We embraced her ma, just as we now embraced Carole Anne into the warm arms of our community. They were family.

So we wished Carole Anne well in her investigation, imparted all the usual nonsense about curiosity and cats, and settled back to gossip about other minor happenings in our tiny hamlet. We rehashed all the births, deaths and imagined infidelities of the males with whom we shared our lives.

Every day Edna Mae came to town, issuing orders to those she considered her inferiors and handing out annoying advice to those she considered her almost-equals. She was also our "family," and that, regardless of the fact that Edna Mae was rather grating upon the nerves, was the real reason we tolerated her.

Carol Anne, on one of her quick visits for coffee, confessed her frustration at being unable to discover Edna Mae's shop of choice. She dramatically announced that she was going undercover and would definitely not report back until she had winkled out the location of the unfortunate store. We all expressed our delight at her resolve, but hid our delicious shivers of trepidation. What would Edna Mae do when she discovered our perfidy. Always buried deep was that long-held fear of her temper when dealing with disobedient serfs.

For about two weeks, we saw nothing of Carol Anne, but now and then we wondered what she might discover in her spying activities. One of our group declared we should give her a new nickname. We should call her "double-o six and a half." She was our James Bond, but without the gun.

A brief note from Carol Anne stuck under the door of the coffee shop told us she thought Edna Mae was sewing the weird garments herself. The gossip around the table that morning was thick with supposition and rumor. If she did sew her grotesque clothes herself, where did she get that ungodly material? We waited anxiously for Carole Anne's return. For days this was our only topic of conversation.

It was nearly a week later that Edna Mae puffed her way to the post office in a garish new outfit. This time the skirt was a green that inspired the dry-heaves, but the jacket was a type of light tan, and something about its color seemed so familiar to me. I was rummaging through my memory for the answer when Edna Mae turned into the door of the postal station.

We all stared, speechless, frozen in place.

There, on the back of her jacket, was an eight inch, blue and red butterfly!

I was delaying my exit from my warm comfortable bed one morning. Looking up at my ceiling, I thought of G K Chesterton's marvelous quote: "Lying in bed would be an altogether sublime experience if only one had a pencil long enough with which to draw on the ceiling." The quote ran through my head all day, so that when I finally sat down at my computer to write, this story seemed to flow from my keyboard.

A FREUDIAN CEILING

The fire in our living room was not serious, indeed only a candle that fell into a container full of tissue paper left over from Christmas gifts. Holy smoke, what a mess! Once we cleared away the ash and vacuumed the carpets, I groaned at the grimy, smoke-stained area on the ceiling. Ah well, out came the ladder so I could take a soapy sponge to the ceiling and carefully eradicate the discoloration.

Good grief! I made it even worse. Now I had a yellow-white area on an age-darkened ceiling. There was no doubt about it. I would have to repaint the whole damn thing!

It took a few days to assemble the paint, the roller, and one of those long poles to help me reach up there. The following day we had a dazzling, clean, white ceiling. I, however, resembled someone who had spent a year or two on a rocky island replete with seabirds that had given me the benefit of camouflage. Thank goodness it wasn't real. With much scrubbing and some serious laundry, my person was free of guano-like decoration.

Something about the ceiling bothered me. It was so—white! I spent days wondering how to soften it. Wallpaper was obviously out of the question. I could repaint with a creamier white paint, but that still was not the solution I was seeking.

That's when I had the brilliant idea of pulling a Michelangelo and painting the ceiling in glorious celebration of some passage from that biblical best seller. However, myriads of damned souls being dragged down to hell by nasty demons would be most disconcerting, and soulful angels with halos and long robes sitting around on boring clouds was not my idea of great art either. Another week dragged by without any inspiration of how to handle that great white expanse over my head.

Then without warning, a 4th of July fireworks display went off in my mind's eye. I had a great idea for my work of ceiling art. I would, naturally, have to erect scaffolding just like Mr. M.

The local store owners were quite curious as to what I had planned when I purchased a variety of paints, scaffolding equipment, and drop cloths. The framework took about two days to set up. Then I got down to the lengthy job of penciling in the illustration before finally applying the paint. The whole job took about three solid weeks, and despite the fact I was lying on my back most of the time, it was exhausting.

When it was finished, I was incredibly proud. Michelangelo's David in fabulous full color adorned my ceiling. The challenge, of course, was that one had to lie down on the floor to fully appreciate it.

The first person I invited over to see my masterpiece was my mom. She had always admired Michelangelo's works.

One look and she keeled over in a faint. When she came around again, she hesitantly suggested I use a fig leaf to cover David's obvious talents. It was only then I realized I had had an exceptionally large dream. I had painted David's genitalia at three times the size they should be,

I figured it was a Freudian slip—of the paintbrush.

Marilyn Kleiber

GROUNDED

No matter how often I think about her, I will never understand why my mother did it.

I was only fifteen the night it happened. I was late getting back from the movies with Robbie and I knew I was in for it. I would probably be grounded for a month because she had been awfully grumpy lately.

All the lights were out and, much relieved, I barely breathed so I wouldn't have to face her until morning. I knew my dad would be cool—he still remembered what it was like to be a teenager. Mom was probably never young.

I don't know why she'd been so angry with all of us lately. She also started smelling of strong peppermint, as though she were covering up something she had been eating. I caught her taking out the garbage one day, which she never did before, and the bag was clinking like glass bottles do.

There was no sound from anywhere in the house when I gently unlocked the front door and stepped into the hall. The house was totally silent. It was odd that Charlie, our little dog, didn't come out to see me. He was likely locked up in my dad's bedroom, but it was still odd he didn't bark.

You caught that, didn't you—my dad's bedroom? Ever since my older brother, Frank, had gone off to college, Mom and Dad had their own bedrooms. They hardly ever talked, and she was really grouchy most of the time.

I didn't turn on any lights, and carefully removed my coat, hung it on the rack by the door, and slipped my shoes underneath it. I padded across the living room, mainly by memory, because the drapes were drawn and it was pitch black. I had sneaked in a few times, so I avoided all obstacles as I tiptoed to the stairs to get up to my bedroom.

On the first step, my foot came down on something soft and squishy, leaving it wet and slippery. I was sure that darned dog had brought in a rabbit or rat or something. He was always leaving "presents" like that for us, although he usually sat beside his prey and panted for our approval. Mom, of course, only screamed and yelled at him until my dad or I cleaned up the offending dead animal.

I didn't dare do that now or she would know I came in late, so I finished climbing the stairs.

Just as I passed my dad's slightly open door, I tripped over something else that was squishy and soft, but much larger than the thing on the stairs. Oh god, not another present from Charlie.

I winced as I fell, banging my elbow, desperately hoping I wouldn't disturb my mom. Her room was right across from my dad's and her door was open.

I thought my heart thumping so loudly would rouse her for sure, but she was already awake. She was sitting on the edge of the bed, surrounded by two or three empty bottles. The scent of peppermint was so strong I could smell it in the hallway. The way she stared right through me was creepy. Her arms were covered in something wet and dark, and at the sight of the shiny, sharp object in her hands, an icy cold shiver trickled down my spine.

I pulled myself off the floor and that's when, in the faint trace of moon coming from my mother's bedroom, I saw what the big squishy thing was that I had tripped over. It was my dad. He was lying on his back, with large wet dark blotches on his pajamas. His eyes were wide open, staring into infinity. He wasn't moving.

Marilyn Kleiber

THE SONGS OF LEONARD COHEN

I search for words in the night
of my mind's eye.
He calls me forth to tell my tale
in voice that rasps
of whisky and of cigarettes.
How can I see when there is no light in here?
I stagger blindly in the swirls
of rough and reedy calls
from his blackest wish.
How can I see when there is no light in here?
My faith will lead me clear
of the fog that binds me
to his haunting words.
For I must find my own
which live only in the light.
How dark is the prison of his song.
the fugues of doubt are fingers at my throat
keeping breath at bay.
It is the trilling note of Bouzouki
softly played
that breaks the spell and unfetters truth
in my hapless soul.
Light shatters the darkest glass
and brilliantly releases my words

Marilyn Kleiber

to join the songs of birds and beasts
and siren calls of mermaids.
No longer in the spell of darkness, I soar.
I soar!

DANIEL MY BROTHER

Jonathan sneaked quietly out of his room, down the stairs, and out the front door. When he got in his car, he let it coast down the hill, his lights off, before he started the engine. He was not going to let Dan know that he had a "rendezvous" with Claire. Dan would laugh and tease him and never believe he could attract a woman like Claire.

Rendezvous! It was her word, expressed so sexily in her cool French accent. He'd looked up the word on his computer just so he would fully understood what she meant.

Dan had always been better at everything and he made sure Jonathan and everyone else within earshot knew it. In school Dan ridiculed his attempts at sports, his academic performance, and even his relationships with his schoolmates, so he learned to spend his time doing his best to blend in with the scenery. He concealed all his hopes and dreams from Dan who invariably referred to him as "mama's boy." Dan was almost a clone of their father: loud, rude, and constantly putting other people down.

Only once had Jonathan made the mistake of bringing a girl home after school. They were only going to do homework together, but Dan leered, postured, made suggestive comments, and told the girl what a loser Jonathan was. Instead of running from the house, she blushed prettily and giggled at Dan and eagerly left with him.

Jonathan was completely crushed. He never brought any female back to the house again. To be accurate, he avoided girls and women at all costs, and rarely went on dates. However, when Claire began shopping at the bookstore where he worked, he found her to be so open and inviting, he eventually summoned up the courage to ask her to the movies. She agreed to a midnight show because she said she had to work late, and asked him to park on the next street and come to the back door so the neighbors wouldn't get the wrong idea.

Thinking about their meeting, he drove close to her house, crept around the back and instead of knocking at the door, threw pebbles at her window. To him that was much more romantic. Claire opened the bedroom curtains and waved. *What did her room look like*? He was dying to know. Unless he could find the courage to be more confident with her, he was unlikely to ever see it.

"I will be right down, cherie," she called.

She called him cherie! Was this a good sign?

He met her as she came out her back door, and holding her hand, walked her to his car. He opened the passenger door and boldly grabbed a quick kiss on her sweet perfumed lips. She giggled and put her hand against his chest.

"Now Jonathan," she breathed, "you must not be so. . .so forward. You would not wish to compromise me? No?"

"Never." The ache in his groin screamed otherwise. *Of course I would. Just give me a chance*. But he was thrilled she hadn't slapped him for being so brazen.

He attempted with great difficulty to think pure thoughts, but when he got in the car, her extra short dress had ridden further up, exposing long luscious legs which disappeared into dark and forbidden places. Forbidden to him because even as his desire for her caused him immense pain, he would not risk losing her simply for the chance to make love to her. That would make him too much like Dan. For now he would only dream about it.

Dan constantly bragged about the women he bedded as if they were all sluts, and all too often wanted to give Jonathan a blow by blow description of his seduction techniques. He despised this in his brother and had no intention of ever giving him a chance to find out about Claire. He imagined Dan's reaction. Dan would push and push until he found out who Jonathan was dating, and then he would tell Dan to "give it to her" because that was all those little sluts wanted. Then he would grab his crotch, do the dry hump thing, and sneer at him. No, he would never tell Dan he was dating Claire.

The drive to the movie theatre for the midnight show was painful, but blissful agony. All Jonathan could think about were the pictures of Claire stretched out on a bed, the halo of her hair on a pillow, waiting for him. Ignoring his visions were like ordering himself not to think of a rhinoceros.

After the movie, he drove her sedately home. His only reward at her door—a small chaste kiss from those full pouty lips. Oh, god, not nearly enough.

For the next few days he thought constantly about her: Claire in bed with only a sheet covering her, Claire's warm body in his arms, Claire in a silky transparent night gown, Claire in...it was no good. He was going mad with the wanting of her. A brilliant idea struck him just like a revelation from above. She would succumb to him with an offer of marriage and a ring. It was perfect.

He bought a ring from a local jeweler. He would keep Dan ignorant of the engagement until news was common knowledge. That would shut him up. He could not stand the thought of Dan's denigrating comments about Claire.

That night, Jonathan decided to surprise her with the ring and again crept from the house. Dan's car was missing. Probably catting around town, getting drunk at some tavern.

The machine gun hammer of his heart nearly deafened him as he walked around the back of Claire's home. He quietly slipped through the rear garden gate and picked up a handful of pebbles. He was so excited at the thought of her delighted surprise when he presented the ring to her, that he could not help smiling to himself. Her lights were off, so he tossed one, then two and finally five pebbles against the glass before he got a response.

Finally Claire came to the window, slid it open and leaned out. With a loud whisper, she demanded to know why he was there so unexpectedly. She did not look pleased. He never got a chance to reply.

"Just tell him to fuck off," growled a voice from inside the room.

It was Dan's voice.

What sort of an article would someone write about their world, if they needed to put a record of their civilization into a time capsule?

WELCOME TO OUR WORLD

I've often thought that if a visitor to my world suddenly landed here in some sort of interstellar craft, he, she, or it would have a hard time figuring out who is the truly intelligent life around here.

You see, there is such a variety of creatures that the initial contact could prove overwhelming. Each group of entities has their own version of a language and way of communicating with each other. I and others of my species understand most of them. But really, a few do speak gibberish. However, they understand each other, so more power to them.

Three groups of us have definite similarities. We all walk upright, we have opposable thumbs so we can handle tools, and we have a more complex language than the majority of those who inhabit our beautiful world.

The lowest group who call themselves "the people" are quite hairy but they are shy and keep to themselves. They are, however, good neighbors and we occasionally trade foodstuffs or primitive jewelry with them. They live in harmony with us and the land and you can hardly tell when they have passed through the area. Did I mention they are nomadic? Even though they are an easy group to live with on the same planet, we don't have a great deal of interaction, because their speech is difficult to understand. I think they even have difficulty understanding each other as they tend to use a lot of body/sign language.

Indeed, the second group of beings, "the hewmaans" rarely see us or the people. Both of our races keep out of their way. I do not consider the hewmaans terribly intelligent. Oh, they are good with their hands, and are very able with tools and can build things, but their artwork is rather primitive, and quite frankly their music is incomprehensible. They have invented a large number of tools including some machines that magnify the sounds they produce, and whenever they have one of their weird celebrations or physical contests, their loudness machines reach into the cool darkness of our peaceful forest. There have been a number of instances when after polite requests fed through one of their own beings have failed to reduce the volume of discordant sounds, we have had to resort to vibratory measures to silence the machines. The hewmaans are unfamiliar with the use of vibration as a means of control, so they always think they have accidentally caused the cessation of function of the loudness machines. I told you they were not all that intelligent.

We are the true intelligence on this lovely planet. We call ourselves "pharees". In our secret language, this means "people of the great world who are one with all". We are about one-third the size of the hewmaans, and about half the size of the people. Size, as you can tell, has nothing to do with the ability of the brain. From the time we are children, we are able to tap into the intelligence of the All, and we can draw power of vibration that we use to create anything we wish.

We are artists and musicians, but our music is the music of all creatures on land or in the oceans, in the flowers and the trees and in the stars and the sun and the moon. It is the music of life, and when we play it, it can even stop some of the noisy hewmaans in their tracks.

We have never been able to figure out if the people have a name for this planet, but we call her Gayan, which means "mother and nourisher of all" in our language. She is but another entity in the play of life in this universe. Her sisters, Ariana and Belaria, are our two lovely red moons.

Oh yes, the hewmaans call this planet Urrth, which always sounds to me like someone retching. They are quite backward in many ways and tend to violence if they do not get what they want. They are barbaric, and while are sometimes capable of extreme compassion and warmth, they can also be consumed with violent rage and jealousy. Their young, however, are compelling, and still connected to the Universal All. Their intelligence level, while young, is extremely high, but as they age, their elders manage to eradicate their most endearing qualities. Most of our deliberate contact with hewmaans is with their young, because they are so much more willing to understand us. Unfortunately as they age, they also lose the ability to speak with us, and come to believe we are simply imaginary creatures. Such a shame, because they have so much potential.

We all live relatively companionably on Gayan, each in our own preferred domain. The people wander from the mountains to the sea on a regular basis, following some urgent instinctive need to move with the seasons. As I mentioned before they avoid the hewmaans whenever possible, because they find that they are treated like animals by their smaller cousins.

The hewmaans prefer to live on the plains, either in their cities where they produce their odd machines, or on lands where they can grow crops and domesticate some of the other creatures to use for clothing, leisure and food (ugh). I have never been able to understand why any being would choose to consume creatures they have lived and worked with and to whom they have given pet names. I told you they are barbaric.

We Pharees live in the cool depths of the forest. The trees supply us with shelter and clothing and much of our food. Occasionally one of the small creatures in the area, with an instinct derived from Gayan, walks into our compounds and offers itself, knowing we have a need for some nutrient they can offer. We always have a ceremonial thanking for the beast when we consume it.

This is our world, and each group lives comfortably in its own area. There is plenty of everything for a long and happy life here.

There is, however, one buzzing insect in the liniment. Recently the hewmaans have invented weapons that fire projectiles for a long distance. They are destroying more of the animal life than they can consume, and we suspect they have murdered some of the people with these things.

I pray to the Universal All that this change does not foretell an imbalance in our system, and a change for the worse in our world.

Marilyn Kleiber

Politics makes strange bedfellows indeed, but the game always goes to he who has the most "toys" at the end.

HOOK, LINE, AND SINKER

The memo on my desk suggested my department would face its greatest challenge from, of all places, the Justice Department.

I was constantly fending off staff-grabbing tactics from various deputy heads, but the Department of Justice was an entirely different matter.

Malcom Beveridge who headed Justice was cunning in the extreme and constantly on the prowl to expand his empire, blood in the halls be damned. If he were also a brilliant strategist, I would have been perusing the want ads already. Thank the Lord, he was decidedly not the brightest spark in the service so most of us had plenty of time to come up with defensive moves.

"Mr. Loftus?" Anthony, my chief secretary peered around the edge of my door.

I raised an eyebrow, urging him to continue.

"Mr. Lipton of Development Research would like to see you as soon as possible."

My eyebrow climbed a little higher.

"From what his secretary said," Anthony continued, "I think he received a similar memo to the one on your desk."

"Indeed. Interesting! Let him know I'll be with him momentarily." I instructed.

I took a quick trip to my private bathroom to contemplate my physical appearance. My mirror confirmed my school tie was perfectly knotted, my hair precisely combed and my jacket wrinkle- and lint-free.

Jack Lipton's secretary was not at his desk but the office door was slightly ajar, so I entered confidently.

"Oh Sidney, thank God you're here." Jack was more than nonplussed. "Malcom is attempting to steal my fifty new researchers and they've been in the department for less than a month. He's on a rampage and pillaging thing again. How can he possibly justify it?"

Jack looked incredibly shopworn. His hair was awry and his tie askew and, horrors, he was sitting at his desk in his shirt sleeves. He had obviously completely forgotten how to maintain dignity in even the worst of circumstances.

I sat firmly in the chair in front of him, taking care to ease my pant legs over my knees. It would never do to have baggy-kneed trousers.

"Jack," I said, "you are looking dreadful. Losing your control this way will not help in the slightest. Pull yourself together, man!"

"You don't understand." He was virtually moaning as if in deepest agony. "There is a rumor going around that this is just the first step to closing my department all together and merging my staff and all the tasks of this department with his. It's some bandwagon rot he's jumped on about cutting costs within the civil service."

"Calm down. If he absorbs all your staff, how can he possibly cut costs?"

By now Jack was wild-eyed. I was most concerned for his sanity.

"He'll cut costs by eliminating my position and those of my three top aids." He was virtually frothing at this point.

"Ah, I see." I paused. "Is there a similar rumor circulating about my Infrastructure department?"

"If you got a memo demanding staff turnover, you can count on it!"

"Then our only option is to prove that his empire grabbing will, in reality, increase costs. Although he is certainly in need of some bandwagon to jump on, I think we shall have to thwart this very ill-conceived idea of his."

Jack raised his eyes to mine and I saw a glimmer of hope, similar to a back-bencher when he thinks his private members bill might finally pass in the House.

"Give me a day," I continued, "and get yourself under control. You are a mess, and you need to be very calm and cool for us to pull this off."

"You're right. I will. Sidney, please, I'll do anything to maintain the status quo."

Back in my very comfortable office that I had absolutely no intention of relinquishing to Malcom Beveridge, I summoned Anthony, my often harried Number One. His network within the service was nothing short of brilliant and it was time to make use of his talent—again.

"Anthony," I said, "I recently heard a rumor that Beveridge vigorously opposed the Prime Minister on his recent land reform bill."

"Absolutely true, sir. The PM was apoplectic about it too. I bet it's not the first time that they've have locked horns."

"Interesting. I also heard a tantalizing rumor that he is seeking the nomination for the Governor General's post when that comes up later this year. Is there any truth in that?"

"Actually sir, I don't think Mr. Beveridge wants that post at all. I think he feels it would be a step down. You know the position really has no power in the country." He paused and squinted, obviously considering his words. "I had lunch with the PM's secretary last week and I'm almost sure the rumor really started with the big guy."

Sometimes Anthony's language is a little too street for my taste. "You mean the PM himself?"

"I'm not sure, sir, but what I think is that the PM is so fed up with the constant calculating and empire building by Mr. Beveridge, he would love to move him sideways to the GG post. A way of neutralizing him, if you know what I mean."

"Yes, a form of virtual castration. I imagine the PM would be quite pleased with that outcome. Thank you, Anthony."

I had the glimmering of an idea. "Would you please set up a luncheon with the PM's secretary for myself and Mr. Lipton for tomorrow?"

"Yes sir. But I don't think Mr. Beveridge stands a very good chance of getting the job anyway. His French, as you know, is rotten. Last month when the delegation from Paris visited, Mr Beveridge told them that he kept his son in the closet."

"Really?" I allowed myself the smallest of smiles.

"Yes, really, and when the French delegate asked, in rapid and perfect French, why he did so, Mr. Beveridge was totally lost. I don't think he understood the question, so he mumbled something and disappeared quickly."

"Anthony," I said, "the French issue is but a mere bagatelle."

As Anthony left to set up the appointment, I called Jack to pass on the news and to ease his troubled soul. "It's Sidney. I have a plan, and it's time to sow some seeds."

"What seeds?"

I spent about twenty minutes explaining the details carefully, with great care spent on Jack's role in our upcoming luncheon with Derek, the PM's chief secretary.

The following day after the traditional roast beef lunch in the Capitol Hill restaurant, we broached Derek with the matter of the Justice head.

"It appears," I said, "that Beveridge is requesting staff from both Mr. Lipton's and my departments. I can only see one reason for this."

"What's that?" Derek was nibbling at the bait.

"I have it from an impeccable source that he so desperately wants the Governor General nomination that he is attempting to appear even more successful and powerful in his current position. Attempting, I would venture, to prove his worthiness."

"I was under the impression he doesn't want the position at all."

"On the contrary, he is quite lusting after it, but pretending to be aloof. I believe he feels if he appears too eager, it will hurt his chances. However, there is a bit of a problem."

"Problem?" He was now testing the hook

"Yes, indeed. Rather than reducing civil servant costs, he will have to increase them quite significantly by adding even more staff to his department, simply to handle the logistics of the acquisitions. It could cause the PM some embarrassment. Plus, if he does succeed in his bid to become GG, all of this would have to be reversed after he leaves. Again this increases costs and adds to the PM's possible challenges."

"Good grief, you're correct." Derek is a bright young man.

Jack piped in. "Yes, and after that last embarrassment he caused the PM, I don't think added problems in the house, particularly with the opposition, will sit well. As for the press, I shudder to think of the challenges they would cause for the PM."

I was quite impressed with Jack's turn of phrase. He had obviously finally absorbed some of my lessons in finer vocabulary.

"You're absolutely right," Derek said, "but he'll never get the position. You know he is absolutely hopeless at French. Being conversant in both our official languages is sort of a prerequisite for the position."

"I do not think that is a problem," I said. "I have it on equally good authority that he is extremely anxious to take private lessons, and is only delaying in order to assure they will be subsidized by the service."

"That would certainly make a difference," Derek said. "But how could this be accomplished?" The hook was now in perfect position.

"Well," I ventured, "I may have a solution for everyone."

"Yes?" Ah, that shining eager face.

"Beveridge is unlikely to get the nod for the Governor General's post based on his past record, unless...unless he is very strongly nominated by someone quite powerful. Someone who would also make sure he gets the French training he so desperately needs."

"You mean...?" Light was definitely dawning. "You mean the PM?"

I began reeling in the line. "Why that's a perfect idea." I said in as innocent a voice as I could muster. "I think you have come up with the perfect solution Derek."

"Yes, I have, haven't I?" He looked quite pleased with himself.

Jack and I exchanged just the faintest of smiles.

Derek was landed—hook, line, and sinker.

Marilyn Kleiber

SECOND CHANCE

"It must be a full moon!"

Sam walks into my office. "What, no good morning?" she asks. "Ooh, Jen, you must be frustrated. The only time you mention full moons is when all the nuts shake out of the trees and start calling you for weird stuff."

Sam is one of my best friends and I rent my office from her because she does all the airline ticketing for my clients. Today she is wearing one of her "I'm a professional travel agent" pantsuits, instead of her usual jeans.

"You're right about the nuts. First thing this morning I got a call from a man who wants to rent a bareboat to take him and his family, including his seventy-eight year old mother and new born son, from Florida to the Virgin Islands and back. In one week!"

"Is that possible?" Sam asks. She does not know boats, being more of a car person.

"No, it isn't. When I told him it couldn't be done in a week, he was puzzled and said, 'It's only an inch on the map!' What an idiot."

"Wow, he wants to take his old mum and a baby, naked on a boat for a week? Eeewww!"

"Sam, don't be lame. A bareboat is not one you go naked on. Although, you could if you wanted to, I suppose. At any rate it's a boat where there's no crew. You do it all yourself. Which was the other thing. He wants to ocean sail and he's only ever done a Power Squadron course. That's like wanting to drive an 18 wheeler when your experience consists of a tricycle."

"Oh, oh, did you yell at him?"

"You know me better than that. I turned him on to a competitor, a woman who's really rude. So I got my revenge." I stop to take a breath. "And that's not all. This morning I get a letter asking for some information on a very upscale yacht, but when I got to the end, I recognized it as the guy in San Quentin that writes to all of us in the yacht brokerage business on a regular basis."

Sam laughs. "Come on Jen, even guys in prison have to have dreams."

"Not on my dime, they don't. I also had three calls from people wanting to rent canoes or kayaks. I don't understand it, my ad clearly says yachts from 35 feet and up. And," I say, "on top of all of that, I had another fight with David this morning. I don't know how long I can continue to put up with him. Marriage sucks."

"I know it's not going well. The weird thing is I could never understand why you married him in the first place. The two of you don't seem to have anything in common. You're such a go getter, and I've never been able to have a conversation with him," Sam said. Then she smiled at me. "Relax kiddo, full moons only happen a few days a month. I'm making tea and I have some really great chocolate, guaranteed to get the old endorphins flowing."

"Chocolate?" I perk up immediately. "Just what the doctor ordered. Let me get this call, and then I'll put the phones on answer mode and be right in."

She waves as she heads back to her office.

"Charterboats, good morning." The man on the phone has a sexy voice and he wants to talk to me. I forget all about full moons. Sexy voices are almost as good as chocolate. Come to think of it, his voice sounds like melted chocolate. Be still my beating heart.

"I'm Keith Patterson, Jenny. Your friend Sandy suggested I call you about handling my boat out of Port Henry"

I remembered Sandy had mentioned her friend was looking for a broker to promote his luxury fishing charters.

"I am calling about that, but I also want to ask you if you would consider helping me out with an upcoming charter. Sandy said you used to be a first mate on a sailing school vessel. This charter is taking place on May 24th weekend and these are some really important clients. Can you serve food and drinks to a bunch of weekend fishermen, and make them feel warm and fuzzy?"

Who would turn down Mr. Sexy Voice, aka Keith? I jumped at the chance.

"Great," he says. "Can we meet in the next couple of days and discuss details?"

Can we meet? With that voice, I'm putty on the phone. We arrange to meet at the convention hall where I will be setting up my booth for the big annual consumer boat show.

***

Convention setup day, Mr. Sexy Voice is due, and I'm sweating like a pig. I know, women are supposed to glow, but for me, today is definitely pig-time. I've wrestled the huge panels of my booth into some semblance of order, put out all my display materials, attached copious quantities of fabulous photos to the walls, and now I can finally sit and take a breather.

You know, sexy voice or not, it would have been really cool if Keith had turned up at 4:00 p.m., like he was supposed to. He would have been in time to give me a little help. I humpf to myself. Perhaps that's not so bad that he's late, because I'll have time to see how messy I look. In the washroom mirror my face is naked of makeup, I have smudges of dirt on my nose, and my hair is definitely not sheveled. A quick repair job and I figure I look reasonably presentable again.

He's still not here. At least the booth telephone is in working order, so I follow up with a few potential clients and even manage to check in with David to see if he is in a better mood. He's not. He's just as prickly because I am out doing something I love and he's in a dead end boring job. Why did I ever marry him? How many times have I sat home with dinner slowly drying like pemican, while he's drinking with his buddies, completely oblivious to the fact that a call to me would have been a courtesy. When I hang up, I'm gritting my teeth and grumpy again.

The back of my neck prickles and I turn to see a man standing there, holding a raincoat. Hmm, he doesn't look like an axe murderer, more like a pleasant salesperson. I always consider salespeople pleasant, because I am one myself.

"Jen?" he asks.

Oh god, it's Keith, Mr Sexy voice himself, and he's got this cute little raised eyebrow thing. My mood lifts immediately.

"Sorry I'm late, the traffic was murder."

I am determined not to drool, so I take control of myself."I'm all set up here, so we could go over to The Harbor and chat over a coffee or glass of wine?"

"Just a minute," he says, "I really want to look at your material. Good looking booth, by the way. I think Sandy has done me a big favor suggesting you book my yacht for me. This is really professional."

"Thanks, but setting up this booth is heavy work, so could you just take the materials you want and read them later? I would love to just sit and relax for a while, and we can talk about your boat."

He agrees and we drive separately to the restaurant.

I am wonderfully comfortable finally sitting in the cool dim light of The Harbor Restaurant sipping on an icy glass of chardonnay. He is delightfully easy to talk to and we discover we like similar music. Conversation flows like fine wine—and the wine is fine I might add—and we discuss everything from boats to travel to accounting and business.

"So, Keith, it's interesting that you are an accountant and are dabbling in yachting. I would expect you to avoid investing in them, because god knows, boats are just big holes in the water into which people pour great quantities of money."

He laughs. "You're right. It would be great to make my living from yachts, but I am more than just a CA. I also help with tax shelters, and investments. So, of course, I have to know about this first hand."

"This is great, because I get so many calls from people who want to know whether they should invest in yachts for charter. Maybe we could we work out a partnership referral thing." *And, I gleefully tell myself, this will give me reason to stay in touch with this delicious man.*

We look at our watches simultaneously. "Good grief," I say, "it's 8 o'clock!"

"Wow, you're right. Look, you must be hungry. Would you like to have dinner here?"

"I'd love to, Keith." *Oh how I love saying his name. It just rolls off the tongue.* "I just have to call home first."

"Okay." He smiles. "I have to make a call too."

Phone calls accomplished, we order and conversation begins again. We have so much to tell each other. It's like trying to devour a great book all at once. It's unbelievable, but I am already besotted with the man, and I know he feels something too. I can tell when someone is intensely attracted.

By midnight we know we have to go our separate ways. We keep delaying and finally leave for our cars, holding hands. *I don't wanna go home!*

He walks me to my car and leans in for the most divinely sweet kiss I can ever remember receiving.

***

Day two, AK (After Keith). How weird I am, thinking in this vein. It's as if my life has been on hold for the last ten years. Existence with my husband has not been good. We're like oil and water, and I've let my sense of worth drop into the depths of purgatory.

Yesterday, I was born into this new life. Today I have found myself again. I remember what I was like, attractive, fun-loving, and enjoying everything to the fullest. Today the world is bright and newly washed and full of promise. The only challenge is that both of us are married. I'll think about that later.

I have only been in my office for ten minutes when the phone rings. It's Keith.

"How about lunch, Jen?"

"Love to." I jump at the chance because the boat show begins tomorrow and I will be a prisoner there for ten days.

I pick him up outside his office and we drive to a great little Japanese restaurant I know.

He has never had sashimi and blanches when I explain it is raw fish, but he's willing to try it, so I pick up a piece from my plate with those darn slippery plastic chopsticks. As I attempt to feed him a tidbit, the chopsticks skid and the piece of fish performs a graceful arc and lands on the back of his hand.

Keith looks at it, bemused. "I guess I will have to eat it now, won't I?"

The two of us totally lose it. I have not laughed this long for years. It is so freeing.

We make plans for the upcoming days. We are both squash players, so he suggests that Tuesday after the boat show is complete, we meet for an afternoon squash game and then go for a long dinner. The air is heavy with unspoken promise.

Keith will find a squash club in town, and I will suss out a restaurant. After three hours at lunch, the Japanese owner is looking fidgety, but he is too polite to ask us to leave. We get the hint.

When I drop Keith off at his company, we kiss again and both sigh.

He laughs. "I can't believe I'm necking outside my office."

"Oh," I say innocently, "is this necking?"

***

I spend the next few days immersed in visions of our budding romance. Then I remember Keith said he has two kids. While I have been close to ending my marriage for nearly a year now, I know Keith will not leave his wife and kids in the lurch.

We speak daily when I am at the boat show.

"I don't really know what is happening here," he says. "Home is so uncomfortable except for the kids. They are both so amazing. My wife and I are really just keeping going because of them. And then I meet you and life is full of possibilities again. It's ..." He was lost for words.

"I know. I feel like I've been living with an unwelcome stranger for the past nine years. I knew I'd made a mistake after the first year. My husband and I have separate bedrooms and barely speak anymore. I hate it. I want so badly to be free again."

"Jen, all we have to do is take it one day at a time. It really will all work out."

I get off the phone and seem to spend all my time thinking about the potentials for our relationship, and finally I decide to go for what I really want. What I want is Keith, and I will take him on whatever terms he chooses. I think about what people in other cultures do and it seems to me that Europeans have a much more sophisticated idea about mistresses. Why shouldn't I be a mistress?

Keith is amazing. I think he's the man I've been waiting for. I'm determined to do whatever is necessary to be near him. I will move, I will find a different job, I will close down my not-very-successful yachting business—whatever it takes. I feel lighter. It is enough for me for now.

***

Somehow, I can always feel him around me, that indefinable presence keeping me warmly wrapped in love. On Thursday he calls me at about 8:00 p.m. and we talk for a while about absolutely nothing.

Suddenly he says, "I've a confession to make."

Oh God, I'm dumped before this even got started.

"Confession?" I gulp.

"Yes. I came to the show today, but you were busy so I didn't want to disturb you"

"Keith, you should have come to the booth. I could have taken a quick break."

"No," he said. "There were at least three people waiting to talk to you. I just stood there and watched you. You looked so beautiful smiling at those people. It was enough for me just to see you."

Damn, this man is so adorable.

We finish talking, finalizing the details for next Tuesday. I practically wiggle with excitement just thinking about it. I will have time on Saturday to go to my favorite lingerie store and buy some sexy underwear.

***

It's Friday, with just four and a half days until our squash game and dinner. It cannot come soon enough for me. I have wasted more paper mistyping and printing before I proofread my letters. Three times I have answered the phone and forgotten the name of my business. I think my brain has taken a holiday.

At 7:00 p.m. I am surrounded by potential charterers when I get the strangest sensation. Keith's presence has suddenly disappeared. I feel empty and very odd, but I don't have time to figure out what is going on. The customers want answers and I slip back into sales mode.

Later that evening, I think about my odd perception, and I cannot recall it accurately so I do my best to forget it and get on with the business at hand. I must have been imagining it.

All weekend I float through the days, happy with the visions of our planned dinner. In my mind's eye I'm planning a house and furnishings and... *Good grief, slow down Jen.*

***

Monday morning I'm back at my office, exhausted from the boat show, but anxiously waiting for Keith to call.

I am at the filing cabinet when the phone rings, and I just about take a header into the garbage pail as I dive for it.

It's my friend Sandy, but it doesn't sound like her. She is so subdued.

"What's wrong, Sandy?"

"Oh Jen, I've had such terrible news."

"What about?"

"On Friday night at 7 p.m., my friend Keith dropped dead of a heart attack on the squash court."

It is some time before I realize I am the one screaming.

***

Marilyn Kleiber

THE FOREST

Daylight fades and the laughter of reckless friends
illuminates our path. We challenge the jumble of trees
thrusting out with leafless arms to ensnare our puny limbs.
We have dared ourselves to enter this unknown place
rife with the tales of childhood trepidation.
We are brave and knowing and so very sure in
our own existence and eternal hold on life.
We are now beyond childish games,
poised instead upon the very threshold
of full-blown, full-grown, young men and women.

The firs are stately tall and unmoving, their reach a prayer
to the stars and the suns of other worlds.
They inspire us to bravery.
Wending deeper into the unknown,
hearing only the endless whispering needles in the wind.
The silence is almost absolute.
The sigh of spruce and hemlock imbues
us with sparks of false courage to delve further
into the gathering darkness.

The flapping of wings stirs the hairs on our necks.
Is this some great owl beginning her nightly
hunt for nourishment? Perhaps a night hawk seeking

small creatures of the forest for her young?
Yet this sound conjures up a vision of large wings,
of massive wings, and an icy frisson of fear trickles down
my spine. What creature waits within the trees for our
foolish band of adventurers? Laughter forgotten,
a sudden serious silence descends and stills all speech.

Hearts beating loudly within our breasts we stand frozen as
he materializes from the mist, long of limb and long within
the cloak he wears, concealing his face absolutely.
He is no owl or night hawk. Instead he is night itself
and all fearful things that inhabit the twilight zone of life.
He is but black eyes, black heart, black soul.
He is not of this world, not of the light
we brought with childish innocence to this dark wood.
As one we turn to flee his presence,
but his black cloak gathers us all.

I hear my companions cry out in fear. Or joy? I cannot tell.
I hear them as one by one their voices stilled
and muffled as if wrapped in fabric no man has wrought.
Then all is silence. I am alone, caught and fixed,
limbs of stone, long neck flashing white
in a silver sliver of moon.
Now cold breath sharply metallic upon my throat,
in shivering anticipation I wait. Such pain!
And ecstasy of warm blood flowing freely
makes vision fade and no fair light
reveals the route to this dark end.

This story was the result of a planned contest submission. The premise was "watching paint dry". I began the story, got totally caught up in it and unfortunately forgot to enter it into the contest.

BELOVED PAINT

The air is bitterly cold and dry on my skin. The silence is absolute as if I have cotton wool covering my ears. I open my eyes. The light is dim, and I'm sitting in a small room. I have no idea where I am or what I have been doing before this awakening. My surroundings seem disconnected from my body.

The air around me is steeped in a strange, almost metallic scent. As I look around the room I see that I am seated in an ordinary wooden kitchen chair. It's that chair that Tom gave me last Christmas. Strange that I kept the chair after he left me. I really did not want reminders of him, but it is a good chair and it seemed a shame to discard it.

I wrinkle my nose at the smell and when I scan the room I notice the floor is wet. Wet? Of course, the smell must be paint. I wonder who has been painting in here? It's only partially done. I wonder when they'll be back to finish the job?

Whoever did the painting must have left some time ago, because it is drying. It's an odd color, a dark brown, but in the parts where it has not yet dried, there is a reddish hue to it.

They haven't done a very good job, because as I watch it slowly drying, some of it is cracking, resembling those riverbeds in the Australian outback when hit by drought. The ground develops into great cracks, with the edges curling up as the earth loses precious moisture. This paint is a little like that, on a much smaller scale but every bit as fascinating as those big, dry mud flats.

There is something gently soothing and peaceful about watching this paint. The red color gradually fades and modifies to its dark brown personae. Then it begins to lose its sheen and flatten like the acrylics I use on my canvases. I love watching my paintings dry too, but their colors don't alter so dramatically. I enjoy seeing the high sheen of my brush strokes slowly change to the flatter, more solid state. Somehow when the paint is wet it looks so insubstantial. Dry is a different story.

The paint in this room is like that. When it was wetter it looked as if it might flow out of the room, escaping the confinement of these four walls. As it dries it becomes solid, and more stable, more reliable. This paint will not take flight on a whim. I can rely on it to stay around and keep me company for as long as I wish. How easy it is to watch this paint. I do not have to do anything but sit here and look. I'm half in love with it because it is so undemanding. How marvelous that it requires no effort to watch this paint as it moves and ripples with the changing colors.

The silence in the room is sublime. Drying paint makes no noise and demands no special attention. It simply is. I am moved to poetry about this paint of mine. I am not sure it is really mine, of course, because this room may not be mine. Claiming ownership, however, feels right somehow. After all, it is my kitchen chair I am sitting in, but the rest of the room is barren of furniture.

Ah yes, I was about to wax poetic.

"Dearest paint be mine.
Do I see in thee a sign?
I think you're really fine.
Oh dearest paint of mine."

I really have no talent for poetry, but the paint doesn't know that. It will bask in my effort to show my appreciation of its attributes.

What's that noise? A buzzing? There it is. A fly has landed in the wet portion of the paint and has managed to trap itself. Foolish fly, couldn't it see that it might be snared in this sticky ambush? It's quite annoying, making all that noise. I am sure the paint does not suffer gladly all that fluttering and helpless buzzing. It is most distracting. That fly has impinged upon my contemplation of the paint. I should get rid of it.

My limbs feel flaccid. I have no desire to move or even to think too much. The fly is safe from me.

"Oh pesky fly in paint of mine
How can you mar such color divine
You flail and buzz and also whine
Coated with paint you'll look just fine."

Oh god, I really am the worst poet in the world. The fly will, of course, be critical, but the paint will be totally allowing and non-judgmental, loving my worship of it, no matter how poor a poet I be.

The little reddened fly's exertions are slowing. Poor thing is dying, I suspect. Serves it right for messing up my beautiful painted floor. I wonder when the people will be back to finish it off? Perhaps they will touch up the place that the fly messed up.

Oh look, the corner over there has turned completely brown, and it doesn't seem to be cracking. I guess it is thicker over there. It's quite perfect. Beautiful dry, dark brown paint, completely at one with itself.

The room is getting colder and the light filtering through the window shades is dimming even more. Perhaps it is evening now. I'm not sure. I have no awareness of time, and neither does my paint. We just exist in space and time is forgotten.

My legs and arms are heavier now.

Why did they only paint part of the floor? How odd.

The smell of the paint is waning. I guess it fades as it dries. It's not a bad color for a floor, you know. Most floors are wood and wood is brown, so a dark brown makes sense. My brain is sluggish and my thoughts crawl slowly, like treading through vats of treacle.

I glance down at my feet at the red color around my chair. How peculiar. You would think they would have painted this area first and so it would be drier closer to my chair. I turn my head to look at my hands but it moves in slow motion. I focus on my left hand. Now this is truly strange. There appears to be paint dripping from my wrist onto the floor. Perhaps that's why the paint is still wet around the chair. I shift my gaze to my right hand and am not surprised to see paint dripping from it too. I am thoroughly puzzled now, because there are no paint cans around my chair. Where is it coming from?

The light is growing dimmer now, and my brain moves like a chameleon, one excruciatingly small, precise step at a time.

Then without warning a flood of memories batter at the corners of my consciousness, demanding access. Unbidden, knowledge flows. I am unable to resist and I remember.

I remember returning to the empty house so I could destroy the chair I'd deliberately left behind. But flooded with painful sorrows, all I could do was sit in it. I remember losing Tom, my home, and all I had ever loved. I remember the sharp bright teeth of the blade. I remember my pale and pulsing wrists, and my yearnings to leave, to end all thought and suffering. I do remember.

Back in my chair
as I fade from life,
at peace,
I am one
with my drying, blessed, blood red paint.

Marilyn Kleiber

THE PROFESSIONAL

Jeremy bounced once as he fell from the roof to the long grass of the unkempt lawn. At least, it felt like he bounced. He moaned in agony as a sharp rock stabbed him in the left buttock. He lay winded, gasping for breath, feeling for all the world like an unfortunate trout carelessly tossed on the bank of a river.

He was far too old to be doing these type of activities. It was his brain that was most valuable, definitely not his physical prowess. After all, weren't security consultants more cerebral than brawn? He was no spy running around muscling his way through the dregs of society. He was a man of fine tastes and sensibilities. No one in their right mind would ever foolishly issue him a gun. So why did she always hand him the most physical investigations? For that matter, why did he always succumb to her directives?

He sighed as he picked himself up from the soggy grass. It was such a rhetorical question. As Director of ICA Consultants, she ran the show and, he had to admit, she had taken the small security business from a two person shop to a multi city operation that billed well over seven figures per year. As he recalled, in all those years he had never been able to refuse those glorious green eyes anything.

"Dammit!" He looked ruefully at the now green-stained, waterlogged knees of his best pair of pants. She had managed to ruin another suit.

As added insult, the man he had been pursuing was a faint cloud of dust disappearing down the back country road. He had only wanted to escort him to the lawyer's office to sign a simple declaration, but Harris had taken off for the roof without giving him a chance to explain. Then, somehow the slippery little character had eluded him.

He limped painfully back to his car and opened the door. The cell phone she had insisted he carry was shimmying merrily across the seat, determined that even in vibrate mode it would annoy the hell out of him until he answered.

He growled a surly "Yes?" into the phone.

"You let him get away, didn't you?" she said.

"You never told me he was half my age, and an Olympic athlete to boot."

"Don't be a fool. He's only five years younger than you. He's no fitter than you, and you're just being grumpy because you screwed up. All you had to do was persuade him to come in, not scare him half to death."

She could be so damned annoying, particularly when she was right. He had slipped up, assuming that bringing in Harris would be a slice of the proverbial cake. He'd forgotten that Harris, like many men who operate in the twilight of the criminal world would, if he felt cornered, fight fiercely for his freedom. He should have taken the time to use financial persuasion, to which Harris would likely have been amenable.

"I'm coming back to the office," he said and disconnected before she had a chance to reply. The problem with cell phones is that you could not slam them down.

An hour later, with his mood much improved by a side trip to his apartment to shower, change clothes, grab a sandwich and small shot of neat brandy, he strode into the offices of ICA, and smooth-talked his way past the hell-cat's faithful secretary Alice, who probably kept more secrets than NSA, CIA, and the FBI combined. He was sure that Alice harbored a secret desire for him, even though his body would never compete with Fabio. And at least, he didn't have the fruity hair.

He walked halfway into the office, his anger resurfacing. He'd lost Harris, but he needed to rein in his temper. He was not succeeding.

"You've got to stop sending me on these junior brawn type assignments. . ."

She interrupted, "You will take the assignments I give you. And," she added as she gave him that thousand yard stare, "I have no idea why Alice always allows you to barge in here as if you are some valiant returning hero."

He glared at her but it was difficult to keep scowling at her, she looked so good. She may be a she-devil, but Maris Black was a fine looking woman. With a great crown of red hair (which would have had Titian on his knees, sobbing in delight) and some silky green outfit that seemed almost pale when compared with the depth of color in those emerald eyes, she was one of the most memorable women he knew.

He deliberately bit hard on the inside of his mouth. It was not in the cards to keep any lustful thoughts in his head about the woman who controlled his paychecks. But she did look good.

"Alice," he said, "appreciates my fine young body, my brilliant mind, and my pure unsullied nature."

"Jeremy Kennedy you are laboring, as usual, under a delusion of adequacy."

She can't be that angry. She only adds my first name when she is merely miffed. Good, I can redeem myself. He allowed himself a hint of smile at his thoughts. "Harris is an idiot, you know. I can still retrieve him later. He just needs a little financial incentive."

"I'm well aware of that. Franklin just located him and persuaded him to come in with the help of a couple of president's pictures."

"Damn you," he said. "Why do you do that? Was I unwittingly playing 'bad' cop? You know for two cents I'd tell you where to put this job."

"Kennedy, don't be a fool. You know you have no intention of following through on that threat."

She has me there, she is absolutely right. He knew the threat was just posturing.

She thumbed her intercom. "Alice, hold all my calls. Call me in an hour when Franklin gets back in from the field."

She turned back to me. "Kennedy you incompetent bastard, get over here."

"On the contrary, Maris, you bitch, you get over here."

The entire city could function for three days from the energy of that smile.

"Perhaps," she said, "halfway?"

We both stood and walked exactly half way.

"Bastard," she said, still smiling.

"Bitch," I murmured as our lips met.

When a married couple work together as closely as we do, it's important to keep the personal separate from the professional. We often do succeed.

Marilyn Kleiber

PUPPY LOVE

"I cannot figure out," Louise said, "how Oliver wrested the cat's chair from them. Normally they're as defensive as hell about that chair."

My neighbor was talking about the new homeless puppy she had accepted into her life, and her two ancient, fiercely possessive cats.

When she found the fluffy little pup, he had obviously been abandoned. The challenge of living in cottage country was that every fall, literally hundreds of small domestic animals turned up outside the doors of our local population, scared, sometimes sick, and always hungry. Puppies and kittens and even rabbits, bought for some child for summer at the cottage, suddenly became inconvenient when it was time to return to the city.

The tiny pup, found on my neighbor's doorstep, was little different from the usual leavings. He was covered in soft curly brown fur, and had huge eyes like the winsome children in those awful portraits that are so popular with old ladies who smell of lavender and mothballs. Louise promptly named him Oliver.

Louise called me over from next door to see him. He really was adorable, lying fast asleep in a basket she had prepared, his belly distended with his first taste of food in many days.

"How can I possibly keep him?" she asked. "My cats hate interlopers on their territory. It will be tough to find him someplace to stay—every home around here already has more animals per capita than any city in this country."

"Your cats are both fairly old now," I said. "Why not slowly introduce them, and allow them time to get to know each other?"

"You're right," she said. "Mork and Mindy probably won't live much longer, and it would be comforting to have a dog around the house."

For the next week, Louise kept me posted about her efforts to get Mork and Mindy to accept Oliver. Both cats hissed and spat at him, and chose every opportunity to harass him. Each time he passed near one of them, a paw with razor-sharp scalpels would open up new wounds on his petite black scabby nose.

He would run to Louise, bleating helplessly, and hide in her skirts. She was unable to effect any mutual kinship between the warring factions. Oliver tugged at her heart. He was such a baby and so unprepared for the nastier aspects of the world. She now kept the cats locked up in one room at night, but the pup slept on her bed, cuddled up between her feet.

Another few days passed before Louise came over for coffee. She told me she had gone to town for groceries and came back to bedlam in the house. Rugs were disheveled, lamps overturned, and her favorite vase smashed on the floor. There was blood on the carpet and none of the animals were anywhere to be seen.

She had finally located Oliver hiding under her bed, looking pathetic, blood streaming from his nose yet again, and Mork on top of the cupboards in the kitchen. When the cat saw Oliver, he not only hissed, but growled in that way cats have that raises the hair on the back of your neck. Mindy, however, was never seen or heard from again. Louise kept expecting to see her at the back door, but days passed and there was no sign of her.

The next time Louise came by, she looked drawn and pale. She confessed that while Oliver seemed to always get the brunt of Mork's claws, she had heard him growling at the cat and chasing him through the house. Every morning, she found Mork ensconced on the top of the kitchen cupboards. It seemed to be the only place in the house he would settle now that his favorite chair in the living room had been appropriated by Oliver. If she tried to get Mork to come down from the cupboard, he hissed and scratched at her too. The only way he would eat was if she closed the kitchen doors and put his food and water on the counter.

"I think poor Oliver just wants to play," she said, "but Mork is too set in his ways. Oliver is also becoming a creature of habit. Yesterday I tried to remove him from Mork's chair, and he growled at me and bared his teeth."

"Perhaps you should consider finding Oliver another home," I suggested.

"That would be so cruel," she said. "I would be no better than the summer people. I can't adopt an animal and then get rid of it if it becomes troublesome."

I was worried about Louise, so when she came by for a coffee two days later, I asked how she was faring with her animal roommates.

She sighed. "Oliver is getting very short tempered. I think all those wounds the cats inflicted have made him cranky. He gets irritable if I accidentally kick him in the night, but he is getting too big to sleep between my feet anymore. I can't persuade him to sleep on the rug beside my bed. If I try to move him, he growls and bares his enormous fangs at me. For a young dog, he has the biggest teeth I have ever seen. You are right, though," she continued, "I will have to find him another home, because at the rate he has grown in the last two weeks, he is already too much for me to handle."

I could tell she was frustrated at the situation, and still missed Mindy. I also noticed dark rings under her eyes as though she were not sleeping properly.

I did not hear from Louise for another week, so I popped over with some freshly-baked cookies to cheer her up, but my knocks went unanswered. Since her car was in the driveway, I did the neighborly thing in our town—I opened the door and walked in. The house was eerily silent.

I climbed the stairs, calling her name, but no reply came. In the hallway outside her bedroom, Mork lay stiff and cold, covered in blood and mauled almost beyond recognition.

Gingerly, I opened the door and peered in. To my horror, Louise lay across her bed, eyes opened in that deep, death stare. Blood was everywhere. Oliver was bent over her throat, worrying at it in absolute silence. I must have cried out because he turned to me. No longer the cute little pup of a month ago, he was suddenly huge, with eyes that glowed red in the dim light, and a mouth covered in blood. He bared his teeth at me and issued the most terrifyingly guttural sounds. I had never seen fangs that long. As he sprang from the bed toward me, I slammed the door and fled back to my own house.

The police were at Louise's house for a long time, and I know they thought I was crazy when I insisted that Oliver was responsible. The fools let him escape. At night, I heard his growls and the shrieks of small animals in the underbrush at the edge of my garden. When I ventured out each morning, I found feathers, fur and small bones in the bushes.

This was not the end. Two months later, two elderly sisters were found dead in their bedrooms, mauled by someone —or something—unknown. The police were baffled and talked about serial killers, but I knew better.

Please, please if a small, sweet furry dog shows up on your doorstep, for God's sake don't let him in!

This story came about through a suggestion of one of my writing groups to present a Halloween story about someone or thing that appears to be perfectly innocent, but is really something quite different.

Marilyn Kleiber

BLAME THE SUN

Blame the sun
If I suddenly seem too light for you to see
or if the shadows are too stark
when I lurk among the trees.

Blame the sun
If the water's lustrous turquoise is deeper than before
with diamond clear shallows as body warm
as the first-drawn pail of frothy milk.

Blame the sun
If my skin glows a delicious gold, infused
with the warm sweet smell of coconut
and salty to the tongue.

Blame the sun
If the vibrant juices bursting from the
fruit upon the vine, sol-kissed, are ripe
for picking and flowing sweetly down your throat.

Blame the sun
For the fields of golden grains and
exploding from their bolls, the soft white cotton
caressing my skin with fluffy fingers.

Marilyn Kleiber

Blame the sun
For lovers strolling through leafy lanes to
bump hip-to-hip beside grumbling brooks
pausing only to share the nectar of their lips.

Blame the sun
For the castanet rhythm of poplar leaves
and soft murmuring and weeping of willows,
their roots drinking earthy moisture from their feet.

Blame the sun
For the tender green of grasses bursting eagerly from
the once cold inhospitable morgue of seeds
where they lay in patient wait for spring

Blame the sun
For the symphony of mating birds returned home
from their winter sojourns to the south, joyously teaching
their young the selfsame patterns of birdliness.

Blame the sun
For the joy of life, for children's happy laughter,
for the dancing winds and thousand sounds
of life abundant on this planet Earth.

Blame the sun
If you find me hard to seize as I dart through life as lithely
as a cat, capturing pleasure in the light beams and the

fondling of the breezes on my body.

Ah, yes for all of that I gladly
Blame the sun.

Marilyn Kleiber

Some of this story did actually come from personal experience. Dating companies are not nearly as discerning as your friends would be.

THE BLIND DATE

"I don't know why I ever signed up for this crazy dating service!"

"Of course you do, Sherry," Jackie said. "You've suddenly become single again, you're a total loss at getting dates on your own and you're hanging around your apartment dressed in your old tatty robe eating Haagen Daz by the gallon. Girlfriend, you need to get out."

Sherry sighed and picked at the remnants of her salad "I know all that, but you should've seen the two guys they've sent as blind dates so far."

"Ugh?" said Jackie.

"Major ugh! The first was seventeen years older than me, but he seemed okay when I spoke to him. It was when we met for dinner that he showed his true colors. He spent most of the time moaning about his 'money-grabbing, gold-digging' ex-wife. And when dessert came, he reached for his heart pills."

"OMG!"

"Yeah, there I am, sitting in this restaurant, having a vision of us on our wedding day. As the minister says, 'I now pronounce you man and wife', my new husband croaks, and out of nowhere, his ex-wife runs in waving a lawsuit at me over the estate."

Jackie chuckled. "So what about date number two?"

"Well, at first I was interested when he told me was French Canadian. I love how romantic the French are. But he had been living in the US for twelve years, so I didn't know how much French charm he still had." She paused. "When he called to arrange our meet, I was a little nervous when he told me I would recognize him by his snakeskin cowboy boots." She wrinkled her nose.

"Snakeskin? Oh that's too funny. I get it you're not into cowboy boots?"

"You know I can't stand country and western music and all that stuff, and somehow I didn't think he'd turn out to be a 'Mr. Greenpeace'."

"So, how did it go?"

"Not good. From the very beginning he grumbled about Canadians and the Canadian government for not allowing him to bring his guns across the border...guns, which I might add, he kept in his glove compartment."

"Guns? Wow, he is a cowboy"

"Then he began complaining about restaurant prices and the selections we have here. We were in a simple family restaurant. You know the kind—standard menu and reasonable prices. I guess he prefers rattlesnake or prairie dog cooked over an open fire, for only the cost of a bullet or two!" She drained the last of her wine.

Jackie rolled her eyes. "Only you could get involved in something so weird. So, what did you do?"

"I just wanted to escape, so I told him I had forgotten to take out my clothes from the washing machines at my apartment, and I ran for my car. Come to think of it, I don't think he had me pegged as the love of his life either. Probably didn't like the way I called him gun-crazy."

"Sherry, you either have to keep your options and your attitude open, or don't accept any more blind dates from Dates-R-Us."

"Hey, this cost me over a thousand dollars. I hate waste and I want my money's worth."

Jackie rolled her eyes again. "So how many more dates with jerks do you consider will be getting your money's worth?"

Sherry laughed. "You're right. Sometimes it is better to cut your losses, but I do have one more date scheduled tonight, and this one sounds promising."

"In what way?"

"Well, his profile stated that he's a successful in-house salesman with Brigg Manufacturing, and he signed up for introductions because he's recently been transferred here from Ohio. He's my age, also divorced, no kids and loves music. He sounded nice on the phone."

"Uhum, well call me when you get home," Jackie said. "I want to know all the details...the good, the bad aaaand the ugly."

"OK will do. Well, I gotta run, thanks for the lunch and for the sympathetic ear."

9:45 that same night Sherry picks up the phone and dials a number. She waits and then

"Hi Jackie—I just got home."

"Hold it a minute, I just have to turn down the radio." The phone clunks on the table. "Okay, give me the juice."

"I was surprised at how good looking he was, and his bod was A-1 buff. I met him at Le Cercle, and he was sitting at the table with wine and a lovely bunch of daisies for me."

"Wow, Le Cercle is really expensive, sounds like you got a good one this time, girl."

"Well yeah, money seemed to be no problem, and the wine was incredible."

"Hey kiddo, why do I think I'm hearing a 'but' in your voice?"

"There's more than one—too many, I'm afraid. He doesn't share my love of art and he never will, and he has no interest in photography. Plus, he thinks he wouldn't make a good father, so kids are probably out."

"And there's your clock, ticking away," Jackie said

"I know! I know! I don't even think there's room for negotiation, 'cause he is so rigid about what he wants and doesn't want. He's not what you'd call a flexible guy". She sighed. "I can't imagine him doing anything really spontaneous. However, the biggest rock in the road is that he has no sense of humor. None! *Nada! Nein!*"

Jackie was laughing heartily now. "Shelley, I think it is time you cut and run on this one."

"Oh, boy, you're right. This is absolutely the last date I will accept from Dates-R-Us."

"Good. Time to move on, hon."

"Okay, Jackie, you can stop drilling, you've struck oil." She paused. "Oh, by the way there was something really rather odd about the date. Quite bizarre in fact."

"What was that?"

"When I sat down, I noticed a white cane beside his chair. He really was a blind date!"

Marilyn Kleiber

ENDINGS

It had been six days since their parents left to seek food for the family.

To keep their minds off the growing hunger in the pits of their stomachs, they relived stories of great parties and exotics dinners their parents had hosted for privileged friends. These were their stories and this their home before the grey ash had smothered their world, blotting out the sun and choking all the green and growing things. Their family's only warning that danger might strike had been rumblings, explosions and fires they saw in the distance. They were not concerned, convinced that these happenings were too far away to trouble them. But the danger had become more personal when the ash began to fall on their home, and their parents had hurried them to the innermost rooms of the house. Then their mother and father left to get help.

Cassie and her twin brothers had heeded their mother's warning and stayed inside barricaded rooms. The water in the tubs and jars was almost gone, and the cupboards completely empty. Their parents had not returned and Cassie was afraid to think of what could have happened to them.

The ash that had settled in thick suffocating layers had at least blocked all the small cracks and crevasses in the house so that no more of the stuff fluttered under doors and over lintels.

The air, however, had become hot and fetid, and breathing was difficult. Their small mouths gasped for fresh cool air. Cassie's heart thumped loudly in her breast, and the fear in her brothers' eyes revealed their burgeoning panic.

She knew their only choice was to chance the cloying taste of ash in their mouths, and the stuffy feel of it in their nostrils, if they were to have any chance at all. Critical thirst and aching bellies drove them to risk leaving the dubious safety of their home.

Cassie layered herself and her brothers with almost every piece of clothing from their parents' room, and covered their faces with woven gauze to keep the ash from entering their lungs. Then, leading them carefully through the house she moved toward the entrance. Every stick of furniture and the fine tiles of the floors were covered in ash, blurring the outlines of chairs and tables. The house had not been the safe haven their parents had suggested. Finally she reached the front door and opened it wide.

The ash, piled up outside and now released by the open door, whispered softly into the house like a dangerous living stream. As she turned to gather her brothers to her, their eyes were enormous rounds of fear from behind their lacy veils.

Moving carefully and slowly, to avoid stirring up the fine particles, Cassie and the boys swam like a small school of fish through the flowing tide in the walled courtyard.

They reached the entrance to the yard, opened the heavy gates, and gasped at the silent grey city across the bay.

All shapes were softened, changed, and unrecognizable.

Pompeii, as they knew it, had completely vanished.

THE PLANT IN THE CORNER

A dusty, fly spotted, plastic Deiffenbachia stood in the corner. Fingerprints marred its surface where people had moved it from place to place. Now, neglected, its sagging leaves remained untouched by caring hands.

He could just see it from his bed on the opposite side of the almost bare room. The plant was the only remnant from the once attractive parlor which had become his bedroom now because he could no longer manage stairs.

He too was old, dusty, and liver spotted. For months he had lain here, forgotten by all except the ancient caregiver who visited just once a day.

He remembered times with family, all long gone, laughing around the table at Sunday dinners, or playing touch football in the yard. After college he and his friends had charged through life convinced of their own immortality, full of juicy, vital life. Three of them had pressed cut palms together and vowed to be friends forever. Where were they now? Why was forever such a short time?

Now, like the plant in the corner, his skin was yellowed with too much sun, his eyes coated and milky, his teeth in a glass on the table, and his bones brittle with age. He thought his friends had lied. Perhaps, of course, they had meant what they said back then, but time had separated them. He was no longer an interesting alive young man always ready for some new adventure. He was spent and tired and his end was near. They might even be somewhere in rooms just like this, wondering why he had forsaken them.

He looked at his sole companion. The plant drooped under years of dust on its plastic leaves. The same dust that was gathering on his old and plastic body—the plastic that the doctors had promised would extend his life. The doctors had lied. Plastic did not extend anything, it just made it more difficult, when the time came, for one's body to meld with the soil of the grave.

He could feel his life force fading in the dimming room. Sounds were muffled and even the dust motes floating in the air slowed their dance. He knew the plant watched him closely with beady little plastic eyes. He didn't care. If the plastic plant was his only companion to ease the fear of dying in a kind of solitary hell, so be it.

The room dimmed and he closed his eyes. The beat of his heart became a slow and gentle thump. He squeezed his eyes and a trickle of moisture etched its way down his shrunken flabby cheek. Alone. No one to see him leave or to hear his last breath. No one but a lonely and timeworn plastic plant.

Suddenly the room was bathed in great shafts of brilliant light. Stunningly beautiful music filled his ears, and his body floated in the warmth of a new and surprising joy. He laughed. There were so many others there, shining in the light. He laughed again at his fears of dying friendless. He was not alone.

There was no death here—just a new and wondrous beginning.

Marilyn Kleiber

CAT

She is Cat
Not kitten stumbling on ungainly feet
not yet grown into
Or hapless target of wretched and unruly vandals.
She is Cat
Not children's furry plaything
with sweet and milky breath
Nor tiny helpless wide-eyed innocence.
But Cat
Lean and lithe and fluid in every limb
A velvet softness welcoming caresses,
but concealing iron will.
She is Cat
In each deliberate move lingers
the confidence of regal sensuality
The contempt of human arrogance.
She is Cat
Asking nothing, demanding everything,
possessing all
Emerald eyes mocking, defying retaliation
from lesser mortals
Remaining supreme, laughter bubbling
from her soul.
She Is Cat!

Marilyn Kleiber has been writing ever since she could put words to paper. She believes that as children we all have the talent to create stories for our friends and relatives. All too soon, our education system encourages us to suspend our imaginations, and we forget the ability to create.

She is published in both fiction and non-fiction, and has a blog entitled" The Writer in Me". Her favorite blog was "Why I write". Her simple answer, she writes because she breathes.

Marilyn has also written a number of short screenplays, and has a feature length screenplay, a novel and a non-fiction book on health awaiting completion and publication.

As a director of Sun Dragon Press Inc., Marilyn's favorite calling is to encourage writers who have a way with words, a story to tell, information to unfold, and a desire to be published.

She currently lives in small town Ontario with a husband, an iMAC, and two virtual cats.